All this has happened before. And it will all happen again. But this time, it happened to Wendy, John and Michael Darling.

Peter Pan chose this house, because in it were people who believed in him. The boys made him the hero of all their nursery games. Wendy, the eldest, was the supreme authority on Peter Pan.

This is the story of Peter Pan.
You can read along with me in your
book. You will know it is time to turn
the page when you hear the chimes
ring like this...

Let's begin now:

You Can Fly! You Can Fly! You Can Fly!
Music by Sammy Fain
Lyrics by Sammy Cahn
© 1951 Walt Disney Music Company (ASCAP). © renewed. All rights
reserved. International © secured.

Following the Leader
Music by Oliver Wallace
Lyrics by Winston Hibler and Ted Sears
© 1952 Walt Disney Music Company (ASCAP). © renewed. All rights
reserved. International © secured.

This edition published by Parragon in 2012

Parragon
Queen Street House
4 Queen Street
Bath BA1 1HE, UK
www.parragon.com

ISBN 978-1-4454-9168-4

Printed in China

'Peter Pan is a boy who decided never to grow
up. He lives far, far away in Never Land.'

Every night, Wendy would tell her brothers stories about Peter Pan's marvellous adventures with pirates and Indians. Peter Pan himself would often hide just outside the nursery window with the pixie, Tinker Bell, and listen to the stories. On this particular night, Peter Pan overheard Wendy telling her brothers some very unhappy news.

'I'm afraid there will be no more stories. Mother and Father say that it's time I grew up. This will be my last night in the nursery.'

Peter couldn't let that happen. He burst into the room. 'Come on, Wendy! I'm going to take you with me, to Never Land. You'll never have to grow up there!'

'Peter Pan! Oh, I just knew you would come. John! Michael! We are going to Never Land! But Peter, how will we get there?'

'We'll fly, of course.'

All it took was a happy thought and a little pixie dust, and out the bedroom window they flew. They dipped and soared through the night until, at last, they were flying over Never Land.

'Oh, Peter! It's just as I dreamed it would be! Look, Michael
– there's Mermaid Lagoon! And the Indian
camp! And John – there's Captain Hook's pirate ship!'

John could hardly wait to cross swords with
real pirates! What an exciting place! Never Land
promised to be lots of fun for them all.

Peter Pan took everyone to his secret hide-out
underneath a big, hollow tree. The Lost Boys lived there,
too, and were eagerly awaiting Peter's return.
Peter introduced them to Wendy.

'I've brought someone to be our mother. She's Wendy,
and she can tell stories.'

John and Michael didn't want to hear any stories just
yet. They were anxious to make friends with the Indians,
or fight some pirates, or go hunting with the Lost Boys.

Peter thought for a moment. 'I know. Let's visit the Indian camp. John, you lead the way.'

Usually, the Indians playfully captured the Lost Boys. But this time, the Indian chief was much too upset to play games. His daughter, Princess Tiger Lily, was missing!

She had been kidnapped by the infamous pirate, Captain Hook.

'This is my plan,' said Hook to Tiger Lily. 'You tell me the hiding place of Peter Pan, and I will set you free.'

But Tiger Lily would not betray Peter's secret.

Flying to the rescue, Peter Pan dumped Hook
into the sea and returned Tiger Lily to her father.

Captain Hook was furious. 'Blast that Peter Pan! I'll trap him, if it's the last thing I do! Now let me see ... Ah! I've got it! I'll kidnap those brats he calls "friends" and hold them here on my ship. Then Pan will have to come to me.'

While Peter was away, Captain Hook captured Wendy, John, Michael and the Lost Boys. The children were taken to the pirate ship, and tied to the mast. They listened as Hook told them their fate.

'Now, my fine fellows, which will it be? Will you all turn pirates, or do you want to walk the plank and fall – *kersplash!* – into the sea?'

Wendy proudly shook her head. 'We will never become pirates! Peter Pan will save us.'

Captain Hook sneered at Wendy. 'So you think Peter Pan will rescue you, hmmm? All right. You walk the plank first!'

The captive boys watched fearfully as Wendy walked bravely off the end of the plank. But Wendy's faith in Peter was rewarded. He swooped down and saved her from the sea. Captain Hook was furious!

'You won't fight me man to man! You always fly away like a cowardly sparrow!'

'Nobody calls Peter Pan a coward! I'll fight you – and with one hand behind my back, you codfish!'

Peter grabbed a sword and landed on the deck. The two fought their duel back and forth, up and down the pirate ship. Finally, Peter got the upper hand.

'Admit it, Hook! You're a codfish!'

'You win, Pan. I am a codfish.'

And Peter chased Hook and his pirates off the ship.

'Now I'm captain of the ship!' crowed Peter, and everyone cheered. 'Where shall we sail?'

But Wendy was beginning to feel homesick. 'Actually, Peter, it's time we went home. Mother and Father will be worried if they find us missing.'

Peter would've liked his guests to stay longer, but

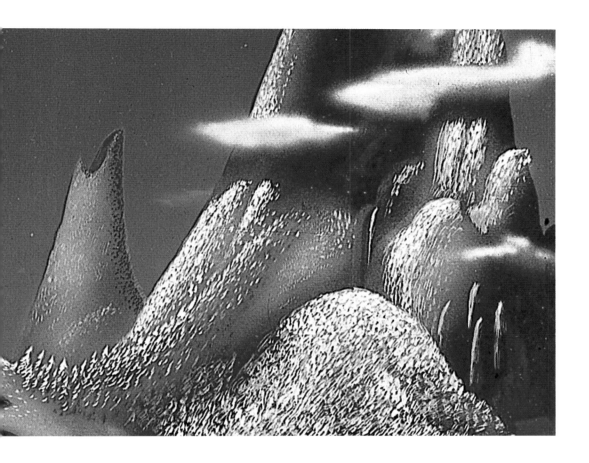

he knew Wendy was right.

'We'll fly you back in the ship. Raise the anchor!
Ready the pixie dust!'

Tinker Bell darted about, sprinkling pixie dust
everywhere. The mighty pirate ship magically rose out
of the water, and took to the sky.

After Michael, John and Wendy had been safely returned home, they watched the pirate ship sail silently back to Never Land. Peter and the Lost Boys waved goodbye.

'They aren't ready to grow up yet,' explained Wendy. She put John and Michael to bed. Then she settled down for her last night in the nursery.

Wendy was smiling as she slipped into sleep.
She would never forget the boy, Peter Pan, and the
wonderful adventure they all had in Never Land.

The End